A Visit to the Farm with Darla - a Sexy Short Story

Dirk Caldwell Romantic Erotic Novels, Volume 1

Dirk Caldwell

Published by Dirk Caldwell, 2023.

A VISIT TO THE FARM WITH DARLA - A SEXY SHORT STORY

First edition. June 24, 2023.

Copyright © 2023 Dirk Caldwell.

ISBN: 979-8223589297

Written by Dirk Caldwell.

Also by Dirk Caldwell

Adventures of Stan
Stan Does a Big Girl and Gives her a Big Orgasm
Stan Does a Female Police Officer While On Duty
Stan Scores on a Booty Call with Barbara
Stan Takes Barb's Anal Cherry
Stan Teaches Oklahoma Karen About Sex in the City
Stan gets Kinky with Barb on Vacation
Barb Wants more Orgasms with Stan before She gets Engaged to Another Man
Stan Does Barbara's Mom!
Stan Titty Fucks Barbara's Friend!
A Stopover in Eufaula to Fuck Lynn Again
Stan Shows a Redhead How to Have an Orgasm
Liz loses Her Anal Cherry during a Three Way
Stan has Sex with a Black Chick!
Stan Has Sex with a Pregnant Woman!
Stan Sport Fucks a Sexy Lawyer!
Stan Titty Fucks Traci's Grandma!
Stan Titty Fucks His Art Dealer!

Dirk Caldwell Romantic Erotic Novels
A Visit to the Farm with Darla - a Sexy Short Story
A Layover in Omaha with Tina
A Night in Eufaula with Lynn
A Trip to the Lake with Kim
Older Women need Love, too! Erika visits Atlanta
Lessons in Love: Gabriella Visits Indianapolis
Big Girls Need Love, too! Barbara from Kokomo
Flight Attendants want Love: Flying High with Jessica
Back to the Farm with Darla - A Sexy Sequel
Redheads Need Love: Megan From New Orleans
A Big Girl finds Love: Joann from Shreveport
Lust from London: My Affair with a British Nymphomaniac
Paula's Sexy European Weekend
Mother and Daughter Threesome

Dirk Caldwell Sexy Short Stories
To All the Girls I've Loved Before: Sexy Short Stories Book 1
To All the Girls I've Loved Before: Sexy Short Stories Book 2
To All the Girls I've Loved Before: Sexy Short Stories Book 3

Table of Contents

Acknowledgment

AI cover image by Freepik

Interior Farm Girl image by Bearfotos on Freepik

Introduction

My first visit to Darla's farm was going much better than I had hoped. Within a half hour of arriving, she was naked on her hands and knees in front of me, moaning and groaning as I was energetically fucking her doggie style, on a towel thrown down on the grass of her rural backyard. We were sweating profusely in the Louisiana summer sun, and she was crying out for me to plow her harder. Her ass looked great as I held her by her sweaty waist, and I was feeling like I was ready to cum but wanted to do her harder. What a dilemma. I reached up and squeezed her slippery tits, tweaked the erect nipples then held her shoulders to pull her towards me as I stroked even deeper and harder into her. Her arrogant attitude that she had when I first arrived was now one of servitude. She begged me to fuck her harder.

Let me back up a little bit.

The Farm

A lovely farm girl similar in appearance to Darla

On this particular Saturday afternoon, I slowed down on the rural Louisiana road and pulled into the drive marked by a mailbox with a whimsical horse head on it and assumed I was in the right place. As I rolled up the gravel drive, I saw her truck next to the house shaded by large oak trees. Yep, I had arrived at Darla's place, a 30-minute drive from the air base.

The night before, I had met her at a friend's party in town, and when she mentioned that she lived alone in the country and sometimes needed help on her farm, I good-naturedly offered that I was not doing much and could help her out sometime, making clear that I am not a farm boy. She accepted my offer right away and asked me to come out the next day, Saturday afternoon. She said she was getting ready for a horse show or something and some chores were just easier with an extra set of hands and a strong back to do some lifting. I agreed, got her contact information and the directions to her place, and told her I would see her the next day. After trying to chat with her some more, she drifted away and must have left the party without saying goodbye to anyone.

Darla was somewhat attractive, and quiet, not talking much even in the party atmosphere. She was a medium-height woman in her late 30's with long, dark hair, but she seemed almost uncomfortable around the people at the party. While my offer of help was genuine and without strings attached, I could always hope for a sexual encounter, but that did not seem likely. I was in for some grunt work on a farm, something I was not crazy about. I'll just credit that as a good deed done for a new friend, I thought to myself.

After the party, when I told my friend I was going out to Darla's place to help her, he told me what he knew about her.

"She's pretty quiet and reserved, keeps to herself a lot. We invite her to parties because she's work friends with my girlfriend, but she does not come out a lot. I think she just hangs out at her farm out in the country. We just don't know much about her."

After pumping him for more details, he just smiled.

"Be ready for anything!"

At the time, I wondered what he meant.

Getting out of the car into the brutal Louisiana summer heat, I looked around the farm. I saw a large horse trailer next to the house, backed up to a white wooden fence. It had several doors open, and horse-looking equipment was hanging nearby, ready to be loaded, I assumed. There were several fenced pastures, a barn, and a small outbuilding, and was complete with horses munching on grass out in the pasture as their tails swished flies away. The single-story house was set back a hundred feet or so from the road and was semi-secluded with large trees out front. Very peaceful.

I was dressed for summer, with a nice polo shirt and shorts, along with polished loafer shoes with no socks. The grass and farm environment made me think twice about what I was wearing. I should have worn an old tee shirt, cut-off jeans, and work boots. It was muggy and quiet, with the sound of cicadas clicking away.

I had brought a small ice chest with some wine coolers on ice, which I got out of the car along with a baseball-style hat with a brim to shield my face from the hot sun. I had seen Darla sipping on wine coolers out of the bottle at the party, so being a polite guy who never arrived empty-handed, I hoped she appreciated the offering. I had no expectations; I was just there as a nice guy helping a friend of a friend. As I said though, there was always the faint glimmer of hope that I could get laid. As I looked around the farm, I could see work in my future but no nooky. Sighing, I closed the car door and walked up to the house.

I went to the front door and knocked. No answer. I did not hear any activity in the house, so I walked around the side by the trailer and called hello. Again, no answer. I went through the gate and walked around the back. "Hello!" No answer.

Then on the other side of a small utility building about a hundred feet away behind some small trees, I saw a female form lying on a lounge chair totally hidden from the road. No wonder I had not seen her. I started walking toward her and called hello again, and this time got a response.

"Over here!"

Fun in the sun

As I approached Darla stretched out on the lounger, I saw that she was wearing a skimpy two-piece bathing suit, sunglasses, and a visor cap. That was it. Some sandals were on the grass next to the lounge chair. I had apparently caught her sunbathing, unaware of my arrival.

As I approached her, I took in the scene. She had a fairly nice figure, with medium-sized breasts and thighs that were sturdy but shapely. I was seeing a lot of skin that I had not expected. She had a nice tan already, which I had not noticed at the party.

She looked up at me.

"Hey, I didn't expect you until later. I was catching some sun."

"No problem, sorry to intrude. Want me to come back later?"

"Oh no, that's fine. I've got about 15 more minutes and then I'm done. What's in the cooler?"

I looked down at the cooler in my hand as if I was surprised by it. Seeing an almost nude woman unexpectedly will do that to a guy.

"I brought some wine coolers; I saw you drinking some at the party ..."

"That's perfect. Hand me one, will you?"

I handed her a cold bottle, opening it for her. She put the bottle to her lips and took a long pull, and a look of satisfaction came across her face.

"That tastes great! It's hotter than shit in the sun."

She looked at me standing there next to her chair.

"There's another lounge chair in that shed. Why don't you grab it and get a little sun yourself?"

I went to the dusty utility shed and found another chair. I set it up next to her, not too close, not too far away. What's the protocol for sitting next to a nearly nude woman you hardly know?

She looked at me without expression through the mirrored sunglasses.

"Go ahead, take your shirt off. You can't get a tan with it on."

I agreed, and a little self-consciously with her watching me, slipped the polo shirt off and hung it over a clothesline a few feet away. I made myself comfortable in the chair and was soon feeling the effect of the hot sun. She watched me for another few seconds as if assessing my body, then lay back on her chair, presumably with her eyes shut.

I noticed that she was covered in sweat. It had pooled at the base of her neck, in her navel, on her stomach, and her face was beaded with the stuff. Then my eyes wandered to her bathing suit. The top was noticeably damp between her breasts, and the waistband of her skimpy bottoms was darkened with perspiration. It was unbelievably erotic, and I felt a stirring in my groin. I opened a wine cooler and sipped it as I lay back, my skin getting hotter and hotter. I could feel sweat breaking out on my forehead and under my arms.

Time passed slowly, with not a word being spoken. She was not the talkative sort but was sort of aggressive, more so than I was ready for. She wanted me to take my shirt off while she watched. Hmmm. Thinking back, she had not said hello, how are you, thanks for coming, or anything conversational like that. Yet here we were almost naked sunbathing together. Odd.

I sneaked another look at her body glistening as she lay there motionlessly giving herself up to the rays of the sun. My groin area was stirring again, and my shorts were becoming tighter and my cock started to swell. Not good, man. I am here to help, not get a woody looking at a silent sweaty woman reclining on a chair, even though that is really hot. I slowly and casually reached down and tried to rearrange my cock so it would not be as noticeable.

She sat up suddenly and turned over, arranging the chair so she could lie flat on her stomach. After shifting around a little, she matter-of-factly reached behind her back and unfastened the strap of the bathing suit top. I tried not to look, but when she laid back down, I saw that her tits were unrestrained and almost totally visible.

Almost immediately, sweat pooled at the small of her back and the waistband of the suit bottom darkened. It was hot, and I was getting hotter while my cock kept swelling. I moved my hand down into my shorts again and tried to give my dick some room. It was getting uncomfortably snug, and I moved it again so it could grow.

A few minutes later, I had to do the same thing again. It relieved some of the pressure, but I was going to be displaying a noticeable bulge soon.

Without moving, she spoke unexpectedly.

"Why do you keep playing with your dick?"

I was stunned at being caught, and I stammered out a reply.

"Well, I was in an uncomfortable position, and I was just rearranging things."

She then had a blunt question.

"Do you have a hard-on?"

She had raised herself up on her elbows to ask the question as she looked at me, and I could see her pale breasts hanging free in the shadow made by her body, the nipples clearly visible. My cock was going to be getting even bigger.

I gulped and decided honesty was the best policy.

"Yeah, I'm getting a bit of a boner here."

She continued to gaze at me expressionlessly, then said something totally unexpected.

"Pull your dick out so I can see it."

I must say that is the last thing I thought I would hear on a trip to the farm.

What the hell? I shrugged, unzipped my shorts, pulled down my underwear enough to give me some room, and pulled my now erect cock out into the sunlight. I'm not sure it had ever been in the sunlight. My cock stood free of my shorts, bobbing slightly, the head a shiny purple.

After staring at my cock for a minute, she raised up, spun her legs around, and was sitting sideways on the chair with her legs toward me. Her top remained on the lounger, and my eyes were drawn to her naked tits in full view. They had a dramatic tan line from the triangular-shaped bathing suit, and the two pale white triangles of exposed breasts were even more erotic.

Shocking things continued to come out of her mouth.

"Stand up so I can see it sticking out."

What the hell. Why not.

"Sure."

I stood up, my dick proudly erect and standing by itself at a 90 degree angle to my torso.

"Stroke it a little." she said.

I was more surprised.

"Uh, okay."

I stroked my dick a little with one hand as it grew bigger. She watched impassively from behind her mirrored sunglasses.

"That's some nice meat. Walk back and forth in front of me so I can see it bob."

I managed to do so without blushing. She nodded.

"The sight of that thing ready for action is making me horny."

I nodded wisely as if I heard this all the time.

"I'm getting turned on, too."

Then she startled me even more.

Arching her back, she took both of her hands and started caressing her breasts as she stared at my dick. After a short time, she took her nipples between her thumb and fingers and tweaked them, causing them to become erect. This was extremely sexy. I was stunned.

For a minute we faced each other, me stroking my cock and her playing with her boobs. Then she reached a hand down into her bathing suit bottom and started fingering herself with one hand while still caressing her boob with the other. My face must have revealed my surprise, as a slight smile came across her lips, the first expression I had seen from her.

"I like your dick."

What can a guy say to that.

"And I like your boobs."

She nodded.

"You came out here horny."

"I seem to be getting hornier by the minute. Must be something to do with seeing a naked woman lying in the sun fingering herself watching me stroke my cock."

"Yeah."

She pulled her hand out of her suit and reached for my throbbing meat missile. She stroked it for a minute while looking at my face.

"I like the way it curves up a little. It's damned hard."

I looked at her as she stroked it some more, then she smiled,

"It'd be a shame to waste such a nice hard dick."

I nodded again. The dick stroking felt very good.

Still smiling, she said, "Do you want to stick that in me?"

"Yes. Yes, I do."

After a moment, she expressed her desires.

"Yeah, me too. I want that meat in me right now. Let's fuck."

I was a bit taken aback by her aggressive attitude but massively turned on at the same time. I stammered again,

"Uh, okay, that sounds good. Shall we go into the house?"

"Hell, no! Right here, right now! Grab a beach towel out of the shed right here and let's get to it! I'm horny as shit, and looking at your hard dick is making it worse!"

Boy, talk about being aggressive. I didn't mind that at all and it was turning me on.

In a semi-state of shock, I walked to the shed in as dignified a manner as I could with a raging erection hanging outside my shorts. My dick bobbed as I walked, while she stared at it. Inside the shed was a beach towel, and I spread it out next to our chairs.

She quickly went to it and laid down on her back as I watched, dumbfounded.

"Come on, I want that hard dick!"

I slipped my shorts down to my ankles and knelt between her spread legs with my cock standing at attention pointing at her pussy. She stopped me long enough to slip off her bathing suit bottoms and tossed them onto her chair.

"Don't need those!"

I gazed with admiration at her pussy that was now in full view and noted it was freshly shaved, except for a tiny tuft of dark, curly hair around her clitoris. My lust increased exponentially, and I was ready for action.

She lay naked on her back before me, her face watching me from behind the sunglasses and visor as I admired her sweaty body. The tan lines around her tits and ass emphasized the pale flesh underneath. It was erotic as hell.

I felt I should perform some sort of foreplay, like fondling her tits, fingering her pussy, or kissing her. My hesitation was met by her leaning up to grab my cock and pulling me to her. She pulled me into position, and as I knelt over her and moved in, the head of my throbbing cock met her pussy lips. I pushed but felt resistance.

She said, "Shit! Who would have thought I'd be so dry when I'm this horny! Sit up a minute."

I raised up on my knees, and without preamble, she sat up, bent forward, and put my cock in her mouth, inclining her head so the visor and sunglasses did not get dislodged. I looked down at the top of her head as she went to work. Having my dick sucked was a pleasant feeling, but it did not last long.

After bobbing her head forward and back for about 15 seconds while she rolled her tongue around and around the shaft of my dick, she pulled back and admired her work. My cock was glistening with her saliva dripping off it and looked suitably lubricated.

She looked thoughtful for a moment, then cupped one of her hands in front of her and spit into it. She then took the hand with the spit and reached between her legs and rubbed it on her pussy lips. I had never seen anything like that in my life.

She laid back down.

"That ought to do it!"

She pulled my cock up to her now shiny cunt.

"Come on! Give it to me!"

So aggressive! I liked it a lot. I pushed with my hips, and after some initial resistance, the purple helmet-shaped head of my rigid cock pushed between the saliva coated lips of her labia and went deep into her pussy.

A moan escaped her lips, and she put both hands on my ass and pulled me more deeply into her. Her cunt was hot and tight, and after the initial friction was pleasantly slippery. I pushed into her all the way, and with our pubic bones grinding together, began a rhythmic thrusting.

After a few moments of silent fucking, she turned her head and looked over to the side as if searching for something, reached around with one hand, and found one of the wine cooler bottles. Taking a swig as I continued to hump her, she spit it out onto the grass as I looked on uncomprehendingly.

She grinned.

"Can't stand the taste of dick in my mouth!"

I nodded like I understood and kept up the thrusting. She took another drink from the wine cooler and swallowed this time, which was hard to do as I was rocking her pretty hard. She dropped the bottle, wiped her mouth with the back of her hand, and started to concentrate on what we were doing. Her face became serious.

"Oh, yeah, that's some mighty good dick! I should have brought you out here last night and fucked you then. I was watching you and thinking about fucking you and got the feeling you'd be good."

I was enjoying the way things were going and getting turned on with the sexy talk.

"That would have been great, but at least I'm here now."

She nodded and her face became a frown of concentration.

"Come on, faster!"

I loved her intensity! I increased the rate of pushing into her and made contact with her pelvis on every thrust.

We settled into a period of pleasant intercourse for several minutes, my hips contacting hers with a slapping sound that I kept up for some time. The sounds and sights of hot sex were incredible. As turned on as I was, I was still getting some very enjoyable riding time in, and she seemed content to let me pound away. The feel of her now slippery tight cunt around my cock was fantastic as I slid in and out of her.

I then realized a few things. There we were on a lawn, fucking on a beach towel, in full view of anyone that walked around the corner of the house. I had known her only slightly before this, and here we were fucking in broad daylight. We both had our sunglasses and caps on, and my shorts were down around my ankles. I had my shoes on, while she was completely naked, except for the mirrored sunglasses and visor.

The summer sun beat down on my back as I worked my meat into her, and sweat was running off me onto her, mingling with hers. I shoved my cock hard and fast into her now dripping cunt. I looked down and enjoyed the image of my shiny dick going in and out of her.

Then she said, "This is hard on my back. Sit up for a minute, I'll turn around and you can do me from behind. You'll go crazy."

"I'd like nothing better!"

I withdrew my dick from her and raised up, waiting as patiently as I could for her to get on all fours in front of me. I wanted back into that pussy! On her hands and knees, she crawled backward to me and guided my cock into her now sopping-wet cunt.

I pushed straight into the hilt. Doggie style is my favorite fucking, and I enjoyed a still moment with my dick buried in her, looking down at her cute ass with me pushed all the way in her. What a scene, right out of a porn movie!

Darla cried out.

"Oh, yeah! I can tell you love it. Your dick is even harder! Give it to me good!"

I resumed rapid thrusting. Really turned on now, I knew I would not last long before I had to cum. I pushed hard enough on each thrust that her ass cheeks jiggled each time, and her tits swayed back and forth in rhythm with the slapping of each thrust of my hips.

I looked down and admired the dark tan line abruptly ending where her bathing suit bottoms ended. Her back had a sheen of sweat and looked great bent over in front of me. Her head was down, staring at the ground with her hair hanging down moving back and forth as I humped her hard.

I could see the thin tan line where her bathing suit top had crossed her back. It was a real turn-on to see that, and the pasty white of her ass outlined with tanned skin on her back shake every time I slammed my hips into her. Sweat was pooling up again in the small of her back, and as I held her slippery, sweaty ass on each side while I rammed my cock into her over and over, I was feeling a build-up in my balls. I would be coming soon, in a big way.

My hands were on her ass as I thrust into her, but she was so sweaty I couldn't get a good grip. Then I grasped her by the waist. It was better, but she was as slippery as a seal. I reached up to her shoulders and pulled her into me as I humped her even harder. Our hips were so sweaty it felt like we had been greased.

She moaned and exclaimed as I rammed it to her.

"Oh! Oh, shit! Oh, goddamn! Oh, man! Wow, that's hard! Keep it up! Oh, yeah! YEAH!"

She was the aggressor in starting this session, but now the roles were reversed. I had her under my control as she knelt on all fours in front of me, holding her by her shoulders slippery with sweat. I was the one that decided on the depth and frequency of each assault on her pussy.

I pulled her back into me even harder, burying my cock deeper into her cunt. She moaned as I hit the bottom of her vaginal vault with the head of my dick. Her ass jiggled and her tits swung back and forth as I pounded her relentlessly. The sound of my hips slapping her ass filled the air, intermixed with her moaning and groaning.

"OH! Oh, damn! Oh, shit! Yeah!"

Releasing her shoulders, I then reached around and took each of her tits in my hands and caressed them then squeezed and teased the erect pert nipples, rolling them between my fingers. At each thrust and squeeze as my cock went deep into her while I played with her nipples, she moaned even more, and I knew her orgasm was within reach.

Rising up on my knees, I pulled her up with me, so she was kneeling in front of me on her knees facing away as I pulled her hard against my sweaty torso with my cock still deep within her.

"Put your hands together behind my neck."

She did, and with her fully surrendered to me, I used both hands and squeezed her tits and nipples as she arched her back and moaned. Then I tickled her clit as she moaned.

"Oh! Oh! Ahhh! Damn!"

I felt fantastic. I forgot about the heat, the sun, and the sweat and was in the zone, totally concentrating on a great fuck and getting ready for the finish.

I pushed her back to her hands and knees while I cranked up the doggie style pounding again. Grasping one of her tits, I reached around to her crotch and found the small tuft of pubic hair near her clitoris. I began to tweak her clit with my finger as my hard pounding of her pussy reached a crescendo.

Darla was breathing hard now, with sharp exclamations of pleasure each time I rammed her from behind.

"Ahhh! Ahhhh! Shit! Ohhhh! Damn! Oh, God!"

Her moaning was turning me on even more. I could feel the build-up of pressure in my balls, and I increased the rate and pressure of my attack on her mound of Venus even more. Squeezing her tit and fingering her clit while pounding her pussy was almost too much for me. I was going to explode soon.

Suddenly, my balls let loose a torrent of hot cum through my erect cock into Darla's wet cunt and I let loose a cry of pleasure. At the same time, she raised her head to the sky and groaned a guttural scream.

"Ahhhhhhhhhh!"

She howled in ecstasy as her orgasm came to fruition. I pushed into her as hard as I could and held the pressure deep into her throbbing pussy while the throes of orgasm swept over us both. After I spurt several jets of hot cum deep into her, I resumed gentle thrusting at a calmer pace, and put my hands on her ass, while she collapsed onto her elbows and rested her head sideways on the towel as her arms would support her no more after the powerful waves of orgasm she had experienced.

After a few moments, I stopped my thrusts into her and waited motionless, appreciating the moment, as my cock shrunk inside her by the second, its work done for the time being.

She lay motionless before me, on her elbows and knees, as the waves of pleasure diminished, and we slowly came back to reality. I could see her eyes closed behind the sunglasses as she lay spent, with her cheek on the towel.

As I came back to the present, I felt the brutal heat of the sun on my back and again noticed the sweat covering our bodies as we stayed joined by my cock for the moment. I was ready to get off my knees but felt that I needed Darla to do one last duty to finish the occasion of a truly great fuck, and I wanted to see how she would react.

I rose to my knees, and Darla rose as well, facing away from me as she had during the last part of our fuck. She stretched her arms and arched her back after the strenuous activity, but I was not done with her just yet. I put my hands back on her sweaty waist and turned her around to face me. She gazed into my face without expression from behind her sunglasses and visor as we both breathed hard. I could not see her eyes behind the mirrored sunglasses.

As her pussy and my cock dripped with the slimy product of my orgasm, I put my hands to her face, pulled her to me, and kissed her for the first time, very gently. She did not offer any resistance. I looked at her fondly and then commanded a final act. Darla was the aggressor at first, but now I was taking charge.

"Suck my cock clean!" I ordered

After a moment's hesitation, she obeyed, bending down and taking my dripping, flaccid dick into her mouth. She ran her tongue around and around the shaft of my dick and bobbed her head forward and back, to get the entire cock and the glans at the head of the penis licked clean.

It was very erotic to see that her sunglasses were still on, and I could see the reflection of my balls in the lenses while her head moved around as her nose was buried in my pubic hair. She wrapped her lips around the shaft of my cock as she pulled it from her mouth, making a plopping noise.

She then sat up straight and tilted her face to look up at me. I reached down to the now-warm bottle of the wine cooler on the ground and handed it to her.

With a grin, she took a drink, swished it around in her mouth, and spit it out on the grass.

"Thanks! Like I said, I can't stand the taste of dick in my mouth!" she repeated as she had before.

"Or cum, or pussy juice for that matter!"

I could not believe how direct and salty her manner of speech was. She took a deep swallow, then handed me the bottle. It was warm, but I chugged down the rest of the bottle as we knelt across from each other.

A nice cleanup

I reached up and stroked her long hair in a moment of tenderness. Not being a tender kind of woman, after a moment she got to her feet and started closing up the lounge chairs and folding the towel we had fucked very hard on.

After evaluating the condition of the towel and chairs, we put them back in the shed. I pulled up my shorts, reclaimed my shirt from the clothesline, and got two cold wine coolers out of the ice chest.

We drank in silence for a minute savoring the cool drinks, then she picked up her bathing suit top and bottom, I picked up the cooler, and we began the walk to the house, me still shirtless in the heat, her still completely naked except for the sunglasses and visor. Well, now she had sandals on.

"Man, that was a great fuck!" She said as we walked. "I was going to fuck you this afternoon anyways after we got done with the chores, but the sight of your boner turned me on so much I had to have it right then! And you fucked me so hard, it was incredible. I never come when the man does me doggie style, that was a first."

Laughing, I said that I appreciated the great fuck and would look forward to helping her out in the future as long as more of the same was involved.

She looked at me as we walked to the house.

"I've never sucked anyone's dick clean like that after fucking. How'd you get me to do that?"

I did not have an explanation, maybe she was feeling grateful? She shook her head. "Unbelievable. Never done that before, and I'm not doing it again."

Then she stopped and looked directly at my face.

"But I'll do it for you anytime. I might even let you cum in my mouth. I've never let anyone do that before either."

She seemed at home in her naked skin, talking about sucking my dick and taking my cum in her mouth. Darla was an interesting woman.

"Thanks, Darla. I appreciated you doing that for me and would love to have you do it for me again."

She laughed.

"We'll see."

We talked a bit more as we walked slowly to the house, still sipping our drinks, and she explained that she was not looking for a relationship right now but appreciated a good hard fuck now and then.

"I don't want a man around except when I get horny, then I want it hard and fast. Then after I get enough dick, I run the man off. Nothing personal, I just like being alone."

"No offense taken. I understand. I'm not looking for a long term thing either. I enjoy sex with you and would like to visit you again."

"Sure, that would be fine. You have a nice dick, and I like the way you fuck me. So, what does that make us? Don't say boyfriend and girlfriend."

As we made our way through the hot grass to the back door, I said our situation could be summarized as fuck buddies or friends with benefits, which would she prefer? After a pause, she grinned.

"I prefer fuck buddies. Come any time. Or cum any time. Either way, I want to do that again. What an intense fuck! Whoa! Are you always like that?"

"Only when I am turned on by a sexy, horny woman."

She laughed and shook her head as I took her hand. We walked into the house.

She looked down at herself.

"Man, I'm a mess. Let me take a shower and wash this crap off me."

"Only if I can join you."

She looked at me funny.

"Okay ..."

We went to her bathroom and straight into a wonderful shower together, rinsing off the sweat, grass, and a little dirt. I told her my shower rules.

"I wash your lady parts, and you wash my man parts."

She laughed.

"That's a deal."

As I washed her clean from the sweat and cum and caressed her soapy tits while kissing her and running my finger up into her pussy, my cock became hard once again as she washed it.

Darla smiled up at me as her hand gently squeezed my dick.

"Damn, you're a horny little fucker. Hard again so soon! Wow!"

I smiled back at her, enjoying her gently washing my rapidly rising meat missile.

"I'm inspired by a sexy woman!"

She stroked my hard dick for a while as she looked into my eyes.

"Like I said a little while ago, it's a shame to waste a hard on."

She turned away from me and bent over at the waist, offering me her cute, shapely ass once again.

"Here, see if some of this this will take care of that big, hard dick. I know you like it from behind."

I entered her without delay and started fucking her from behind, the warm water and slippery, clean soapy bodies acting as an aphrodisiac. My blood was boiling, and I was horny as ever very quickly. I ran my hands over her tits as I pounded her from behind, playing with the nipples and then rubbing her clit.

While I was banging away at her sweet ass, I looked down and admired her asshole with soap suds dripping over it. I started to form an idea. I then took a soapy finger and ran it around the dark skin of her exposed, wrinkled, asshole a few times, applying a little pressure to the anus but not penetrating her. While she moaned appreciatively a few times, I could tell she would not come again.

I wouldn't have minded fucking her in the ass right then, but I would never surprise a woman by just sticking my cock up her ass. There are things a gentleman simply does not do without permission. Besides, my mind was set on coming inside her pussy again very soon, and I concentrated on holding out as long as I could. I was in the moment, with the warm water splashing down on us the whole concept of shower fucking made this a very enjoyable interlude.

After a few more minutes of frenzied humping, I came inside her, shooting load after load of hot cum deep into her tight, slippery cunt. I pushed in all the way and held that as my dick started to shrink and the last ounce of cum dribbled out. I almost fell to my knees as the wave of euphoria washed over me.

Pulling out, and my knees were shaking as Darla turned around and gently washed my dick with her hands and rinsed me off. I helped out by washing her shaved, slippery pussy with a free hand. It was a gentlemanly thing to do.

As we got out of the shower and toweled off in companionable silence, she surprised me by bending down and taking my cock in her mouth again. After a few minutes of very enjoyable tongue action, as I leaned up against the bathroom sink, she raised up and gave me a shy smile.

"I didn't mind the taste of your dick that time," she said quietly. "Maybe I'm getting used to it. We'll have to try it again sometime."

I told her I agreed with that concept and looked forward to the opportunity. She then surprised me further.

"I just might let you fuck me in the ass some time. I've never let anyone do that before either. I know you wanted to."

Surprised and speechless, I bent over and kissed her as she held my limp dick in her hand.

"I'd like that very much, just let me know when you are ready."

Then she looked at me and smiled.

"What the hell is it with you? I've told you that you could come in my mouth and now I am going to let you have anal sex with me. You make me want to try new things!"

I laughed and said it must be my smile because we hadn't talked that much yet.

"Who's got time to talk when there's fucking to be done? Anyways, get your clothes on, we still have work to do outside. Or have you forgotten why you came out here today?"

I had not forgotten but was secretly hoping she had.

Getting to work

We got dressed, me in the date clothes I had with me, and Darla in a purple tank top and cutoff jeans shorts. I noticed she did not bother with a bra under the tank top, which I appreciated as we walked out to the barn. Her medium-sized boobs had a nice bounce as she walked, and the top was cut low enough that I got a good view of her medium sized boobs.

Once at the barn, she had me busy lifting and arranging feed sacks, saddles, and assorted horse stuff. She and I would lift some items together, and for others, I was on my own. We both were sweating profusely in the humid Louisiana summer afternoon. After a half hour of work, she came to a point where she needed to hook her truck up to the horse trailer and back it near the barn to load stuff we had positioned.

We walked back to the truck, which was next to the house. She got us each a bottle of water and explained that it would be easier to connect the truck if I guided her back from near the trailer hitch, which was a device called a gooseneck. I had never seen one before.

As she climbed into the truck cab, she was telling me to do something that I could not hear over the sound of the truck engine. I moved closer to her as she sat in the driver's seat, and standing next to her could not resist getting a feel of her boobs through the tank top.

I put a hand on her bare leg, then cupped a boob in my hand as she looked at me with a smile.

"Still horny? You just came about a half hour ago. Man, you are some kind of stud. What are we doing?"

I couldn't think of a good answer, so I said something to the effect of truck fucking or something like that. She nodded as if she understood.

She shut off the truck and got out, reaching behind the seat for a blanket. We then walked to the open tailgate of the truck, where she spread out the blanket on the tailgate. She climbed up on it and grinned at me.

"Okay, stud. Have at it! Do whatever you want!"

I pulled her tank top off, revealing her nice naked boobs. I kissed each one in turn and nibbled on the nipples, getting a moan from her. I then unfastened and pulled off her shorts, noticing there was no underwear impeding me.

"No panties? What were you planning on, Darla?"

She grinned again.

"You caught me. I figured you would be wanting back in my pants, so I skipped the panties. Do you mind?"

"Hell, no. I like pussy in the raw."

She giggled and I ran a finger over her hairless labia, again noticing the tuft of dark hair over her clit.

"What's up with the little bush around your clit?"

She laughed.

"That's so most men can find the thing. You don't seem to have that problem."

I spread her legs and stood between them, then bent over and gave the bearded clit a kiss, then licked it. She moaned in appreciation, and I continued down her slit, licking the inside of the lips and ending up at the hole of the vaginal vault.

Sticking my tongue in her hole, I enjoyed the smell of hot pussy. We had bathed, but I had fucked it since then, so I belatedly thought there might be residual cum still inside. I went back to the clit, still relishing the aroma of cunt.

After giving the clit some love, I put a finger in her and searched for her G spot. Once I was on it, she drew in a sharp breath, then moaned as I massaged it. Her hips squirmed, so I knew I was in the right area. I then went up to her chest and caressed her boobs, tweaking and squeezing the nipples. Putting my mouth to work, I sucked on each nipple and gave each a nibble as she moaned, and her hips continued to squirm.

I stopped for a moment to take my shirt off and dropped my shorts, stepping out of them. Now we were both naked, and although out of view of cars passing by, anyone coming up the driveway would see us. At least we were in the shade.

She put her hand on my dick and stroked it as I went back to her boobs and pussy. She had her head back and eyes closed as I worked her over, and her moaning was on the increase. I slide her ass closer to the edge of the tailgate so I could reach her while I was standing on the ground. The tailgate was at a great height for straight fucking, but for doggie style, I would have to find a different spot.

I put the head of my stiff cock up to her labia.

"Put me in you!" I commanded, wanting to be the aggressor on this round.

She reached for me and pulled me to her, with her pussy wet enough from my licking and her juices that she got the head in without any issues.

"Deeper! Climb onto my dick!"

She scooted closer to me and as my cock went in her, moaned with pleasure.

"Oh, shit! That feels good!"

"Wrap your legs around me, tight!"

She did so, and I gave a few thrusts to get in all the way, then put my hands under her ass and lifted her off the tailgate, with her impaled on my dick. She squealed with pleasure and apprehension.

"Wow! That's in deep! What are you doing?"

By way of an answer, I moved around to the side of the truck and leaned her up against the side and commenced to fucking her hard. She groaned and moaned as I put the meat to her, with her sweaty back up sliding against the truck.

"Oh! Damn! Oh, shit! Wow!"

After a minute of that, I carried her to the open door of the truck, where I set her down on the edge of the bench seat and went back to fucking her hard.

She was groaning loudly now, and with her legs wrapped tight around me and her arms around my neck she was able to push her hips into me as I pounded into her. Fucking her on the edge of the seat was fun, and she responded.

"Oh! Oh! Ah, damn! Oh!"

I then pulled her off the seat, and slowly going to the ground next to the truck, went to my knees in the grass while still bouncing her on my dick. It felt fantastic.

After giving her a few strokes holding her up while she clung to me, I laid her on her back in the grass and fucked her for a minute like that as she groaned. Then I raised up and told her to get up and bend over the truck tailgate.

"Oh, wow! Okay!"

She scrambled to get up and went with me to the rear of the truck, where she assumed the position, bent over the tailgate with her elbows on the blanket we had started out on. I put my feet outside of hers as she reached between her legs for my cock, which was in position at the entrance to her hole.

I pushed deep into her and started a hard fuck again while I held her ass with one hand while fondling her boobs with the other. My hips were slapping her ass, jiggling her butt cheeks and boobs. She was vocal in her approval of the position and rate of copulation.

"Oh, goddamn! Son of a bitch, that's good! Yeah! Yeah! Oh, yeah!"

A few minutes of fast fucking later, I reached for her clit with one hand and tickled it with my forefinger as she cried out, and then circled her brown, wrinkled anus with my other forefinger. She like it a lot.

"Oh, shit! Oh, fuck! Oh! Oh! Ahhhhh! I'm coming! ERRRAAAGGHHH!"

She let out a yell of passion as she came, and I was right behind her. I came in a rush, shooting wave after wave of hot cum into her as she shuddered, in the throes of orgasm.

I stopped, and we stayed in position for a minute, my cock still inside her, our breath ragged and fast, while my knees shook with reaction.

After an interval, I pulled out of her and stepped back, still shaky. She turned around to me, then I put my arms around her as she recovered. She in turn put her arms around me and caressed my ass and stroked my hair while we stood together with her head on my chest, both dripping wet from exertion in the hot afternoon.

She was the first to speak, as she tilted her head to look at me.

"I guess we wasted that shower earlier. What the hell got into you? Did you just get out of prison or something?""

I shrugged.

"Purple tank tops with nice boobs and no bra really turn me on." She laughed.

"I'll keep that in mind not to wear that when there is work to be done. Whew! I've never been fucked like that before. On the tailgate, up against the truck, on the seat, in the grass, then doggie style over the tailgate... that's a lot of fun. You really know how to mix things up."

We were standing naked next to the truck now, easily visible from the road. A car went by, hopefully they did not see us.

She was shaking her head.

"And you've made me come twice now fucking me doggie style. That never happens with me. What is it about you?"

I smiled, having cum three times in a row fucking her from behind.

"I had lessons when I was younger on clitoral stimulation."

She laughed.

"You remembered them pretty well! Son of a bitch, that was good!""

I gave her sweaty boobs a final squeeze.

"Shall we get dressed?"

She nodded.

"Maybe if you can control yourself, we can actually hook up the damned truck now."

Then she looked at herself and shook her head.

"I need to hose off some of this dirt and cum before I put my shorts back on. Come on. Let's go to the shed."

We walked naked to the shed about a hundred feet away. She hosed off with the cool water, and as I watched, she directed the stream of water up into her pussy, rinsing it clean. I was mesmerized. I rinsed off as well. She had a barn towel handy to dry off with. We dressed and went back to the truck. She climbed into the cab.

"Okay, let's try this again. Watch the hitch as it comes over the ball, then point which way you want me to go."

"Okay."

She backed up slowly, and after a few tries, we got the hitch over the ball.

"Now turn the crank over there to lower the trailer onto the ball."

With that done, she had me push a lever, and the trailer was locked onto the ball.

"Now we back the trailer next to the barn. Make sure I don't hit anything."

She skillfully backed the trailer next to the barn. Shutting the truck off, we then loaded the supplies, feed sacks, and the other horsey crap into various compartments on the trailer.

After that was done, we went to the house and sat in the kitchen, resting.

Darla announced, "I'm tired, we can finish the rest of this tomorrow."

I just looked at her.

"Are you implying I'm going to help you again tomorrow?"

She smiled and laughed.

"Yeah, I figured we could clean up and then take your car into town and get something to eat. After that, it's your call on what you want to do. If you can help me tomorrow it would be great, and you'll probably want to get in my pants again anyway even though you've cum about three times already."

"You're a mind reader about me wanting back in your pants. Okay, let's take my car to town and play it by ear after that."

She nodded.

"I just need to feed the horses before we go. Come on, you can help with the watering. It'll go faster if you can keep your hands off me. You'll have to wait until later, if you can even get it up again."

"I make no guarantees about that, but I'll help with the watering."

Dinner in Town

Darla fed the beasts, and I hauled water to the buckets in each stall. Back at the house, she took several minutes and changed clothes into a white pleated short golf skirt and another tank top, this one a silky pale blue which was tighter and showed off her unrestrained boobs. She wore dangly earrings, a necklace, and a watch for jewelry. Some makeup had been added around her eyes.

I admired the outfit when she emerged from her bedroom.

"Nice! Your legs and ass look good, and your boobs are well displayed for all to see."

She smiled shyly.

"Thanks, I think my thighs are too big and fat. I figured you would like the braless look with this top."

I put my arms around her.

"You figured correctly. I like the way you look, it's sexy. Your legs look fine, and you know I love getting between them. Thanks for dressing nice for me."

She blushed and turned away.

"Let's go, you're embarrassing me. We can talk about my idea of where to eat on the way."

On the way back south on Louisiana Highway 3, it was about 15 minutes to the small town of Benton, then about 15 more minutes to Bossier City and Shreveport. On the way, she was quiet for several minutes, then brought up some ideas about dinner.

"How long have you been in Shreveport?"

"Long time. About six or seven years now."

She shook her head.

"Damn, we could have been fuck buddies this whole time!"

I had to laugh.

"I have missed out on a lot of Darla fun."

"No shit. Why I was asking, have you been to Johnnie's Pizza?"

"Yeah, it's pretty good."

"How about we go and eat there and then you can take me back to the house?"

I nodded.

"That's fine."

She was quiet for a while, then had an idea.

"See that convenience store up there on the left? Pull in, they have great frozen daiquiris to go. We can drink on the way to Johnnie's."

"Sounds good."

I'd have to be careful; I did not want to get a career-ending DUI just to have a good time. We both got drinks. I got a small, she got a large.

She said, "I'll pay for drinks tonight. You can get the pizza."

As we were getting into Bossier City and a couple of minutes from the pizza place, she asked for my hand.

"Give me your hand."

I did, and she slid it up under her golf skirt, which is how I found out she did not have panties on. She directed my hand to her shaved pussy, looked at me and smiled.

"This will give you something to think about during dinner."

"Nice!"

I played with her pussy a little, tracing the labia with my finger and slightly entering her. She looked disappointed.

"Finger me a little more. We're almost there."

"Wait until later, Miss impatient."

I tickled her clit with the tuft of hair just as we pulled in. She looked happier.

"That's a little better. I was afraid you didn't like me anymore."

"Don't worry, my wacky fuck buddy. I still like you and want more of that later."

She grinned.

"Damn, I hope so. It's been at least an hour since we had sex."

As we got out of the car, she slurped the last of her drink. She was really pounding that down, and we were both dehydrated and hungry.

Just before we went in, she stopped me and took my right hand, then she sucked on the finger that had been in her vagina. She grinned.

"Wanted to clean you up before we went in."

"I think you're a little drunk already, my girl."

She laughed.

"Maybe just a little …"

We ordered, and she got a beer for each of us. While we were waiting for the pizza, she drank all of her beer and half of mine. She was getting a little loopy and loud but laughing and having a good time. I got the impression she did not get off the farm much except to go to work.

After we ate, she wanted to stop back at the convenience store and get another frozen daiquiri. Her speech was getting slurred, even after eating.

"They are soooo good when it's hot like this! Hey, you haven't finished your small one. I'll get you a large, if you want you can drink it when we get back to my place."

"That's what I'll do. I don't want a DUI."

"You are a very, very smart man. That's why I like you. Well, that and you have a tasty dick."

She was hammered, and it was going to get worse as she finished her big drink. I shrugged. She wasn't driving and felt safe enough with me to get loaded.

It was getting dark, and she decided it was time for show and tell.

"Do you want to look at my boobs?"

I glanced over as she pulled her shirt up and showed them off.

"Nice! I'll look at them more when we aren't driving."

She took my hand and put it on one of them. It felt pretty nice.

"There! You can appreciate them and not have to look."

"Very good idea. I like playing with them."

She giggled.

"And they like playing with you. Hey! Why don't you pull over and we'll have sex in the car."

"I'd rather get to your place and do it on something comfortable."

She nodded.

"Very, very smart man, I'm telling ya. Okay, we'll wait. But you can finger me and drive, can't you?"

"I think so."

She moved my hand to her pussy and spread her legs.

"There ya go! Finger away."

I turned to her road from the highway. Five miles to go and little traffic. I could do a little fingering.

After a minute of nice fingering and getting some moans out of her, she decided I needed better access and turned her ass to me as she laid back on her seat, and with some effort put one foot in front of the steering wheel on the dashboard, and the other behind my neck, resulting in her being spread-eagled with her crotch facing me sideways in a moving car. It was incredibly awkward to drive like that, not to mention distracting. But I had good access.

"There! That way you can get to everything!"

I had to laugh.

"Darla, you crazy ass drunk! I can barely see! Just wait a minute, we'll be at your driveway soon if I can stay on the road."

She laughed delightedly.

I managed to stay on the road somehow, pulled into her driveway, and shut the car off. She was still spread out and was giggling. I pulled my finger out and opened my door when she stopped me.

"Kiss my pussy while I'm all spread out! It'll be cool!"

"Okay, you wacky drunk sexpot."

I leaned back into the car, which was now illuminated by the door being open, bent down, and gave her pussy a few kisses and licks, even sticking my tongue into her hole, which she responded to by groaning.

I then rose, shut my door, and went to try and get her out of the car. It was a task, as she had her legs on the wrong side to get out. I ended up taking her under the arms and pulling her out while she was laughing her ass off.

"That did not turn out to be the most graceful thing I've ever done!"

I was laughing with her.

"But it was interesting. Can you walk?"

"Of course! Oops! Maybe you can help me."

I took her arm as she staggered to the door, and after we got in and turned a light on, she went straight to the couch and flopped down.

"Whew! I'm just a little tipsy. It may have been because of two large daiquiris and a beer."

"And now I can have my drink and catch up to you. Am I staying the night?"

"Oh, fuck yeah. That way we can do it all night!"

I had to laugh.

"I don't think you will be awake long enough to do it once."

"We'll see, smart ass. Do you want to sit down and kiss me?"

I was surprised.

"I didn't know you liked to kiss."

"Oh, sure I do. But usually only when I have had a few drinks, then I get to feeling romantic. Usually, I don't give a shit about kissing."

"I understand. I'll be happy to kiss you."

"Good! I kiss better without my shirt on!"

With that, she pulled her tank top off, exposing her nice boobs.

"I'm inspired."

I leaned in and started kissing, which she was surprisingly good at. I cupped a naked boob with my hand and started caressing it. She moaned in her throat as I kissed her deeply, our tongues searching each other's mouths. After a minute, she pulled back and grinned.

"That's good kissing! And you taste kind of salty. Is that pizza or my pussy since you had your tongue up there?"

"It might be a little of both."

"That's cool. Later, I want you to kiss me right after you've had your tongue up my pussy so I can see what you are tasting."

"Okay, crazy lady."

She giggled again.

"Crazy drunk horny lady!"

"I stand corrected."

"You are so funny. Are you going to fuck me right here on the couch?"

"I don't want to take advantage of you while you are drunk, Darla."

"Shit, I'm not that drunk. Besides, so far, you've already fucked me on a towel on the ground, in the shower, and standing up against my truck. It's not like it's a surprise."

I had to laugh.

"I see your point."

"Exactly! Let's go to the bedroom, though. If I pass out after, I'm in the right spot."

"Very practical. Okay, let's go."

We changed venues to the bedroom, and she lay on the bed in a suggestive pose, smiling sweetly.

"Darla, that would be more effective with your shoes off."

"Oh, yeah. How's that?"

"Beautiful. It makes me want to come make passionate love to you right now."

"What's stopping you?"

I took off the clothes I had on and stood next to the bed.

"How about some head, with you on all fours facing me?"

She grinned as she got the idea,

"Like a doggie-style blow job? Okay!"

She got on all fours and faced my semi-erect dick, then put her head to the proper angle for entry and started sucking me. It felt great. She took me down her throat to the gagging point and backed off enough to make it very pleasurable.

"Oh, Darla. That feels great!"

She pulled back and smiled.

"I don't mind your dick anymore, it's the strangest thing."

"You're in a romantic mood."

"I guess so. Can you kiss me and finger me some more before you fuck me?"

"I would be honored."

She giggled and moved up on the bed.

I started kissing her and fondled a boob with one hand while I put the other under her skirt and started fingering her. As soon as I slipped my finger in, she started groaning. I massaged her G spot and got her hips squirming as our tongues intertwined. She pulled back.

"Do you want to take my skirt off?"

"No, I think it's sexy to do it this way."

"All right, just try not to get cum on it."

"Yes, Ma'am."

We went back to kissing and after a minute she pulled back again.

"If I pass out, you have my permission to fuck me."

"Okay, but gentlemen don't have sex with unconscious partners."

"That's so nice. That's why I like you, otherwise with most men I'd wake up with cum in my mouth, pussy, and asshole."

I had to laugh.

"I try to live to higher standards than that."

"Oh, you are really nice. Go ahead and fuck me now, please."

I kneeled between her legs and put my cock against her labia. She took a hand and wiggled the head to just the right position.

"Okay, push. Slide that fucker in there!"

I started laughing again. She looked at me as I shoved my cock in her.

"What? Did I say something funny?"

"Oh, Darla. You are so wasted. I hope you remember this in the morning."

She looked puzzled.

"I don't know why I wouldn't."

Starting and nice, easy rhythm of thrusting into her, she started moaning and commenting at the same time.

"Oooooh! Oh, yeah! Give me that dick, you fucker! Oh yeah! C'mon, do it! Mmmm!"

I was cracking up while banging away on her.

"You are so funny, my girl!"

"Yeah! I have been wanting your dick like all day! Give it to me!"

"Darla, honey? We've already done it three times today."

She looked puzzled again.

"We did? Good for us, horny little fuckers that we are. In that case, give it to me again, you fucker! Why are you laughing? Pay attention and give me that dick!"

"Yes, dear."

She patted my ass as I pushed into her.

"Atta boy!"

After a while, I noticed she was just lying there.

"Darla? Are you awake? Would you like to participate in this event by maybe pushing your hips into me?"

"Oh, yeah. Sorry, I was getting sleepy. Here ya go!"

She energetically pushed her hips into me and moaned loudly.

"Oh, man! I think that did it! I'm coming! I think I'm coming. Yeah, definitely coming! Ohhhh! Shit! Fuck! Ahhhhh!"

She arched her back and let loose a shout of pleasure. I was glad the nearest neighbors were far away. I felt her body shudder and then relax as the orgasm went through her.

"Whew! That was nice. Did you come yet?"

I was pounding away on her.

"Still working on it, my dear."

"Well, lift my legs up and get deep. You should like that. Or do you want to fuck me in the ass now?"

I lifted her legs and cranked up the pressure and rate of pounding, hearing the slap of flesh against flesh that I loved to hear.

"I'll do your ass another time when you're sober."

She gasped out, "Okay!"

She closed her eyes and hung onto my arms.

"Oh, that's good! Give it to me good, you fucking stud! Damn, I'm glad I met you! Ohhhh! Shit! That's good fucking! Wow!"

I moved her ankles over my shoulders and had her pussy exposed to my merciless pounding. She grimaced and groaned as I put the meat to her as hard as I could. She seemed to enjoy it.

"Ohhhh! God damn! Oh, shit! Ahhhhhh! That's it! Come on, you fucker! Ohhhh, shit! Oh, damn, that's good! Give me that cum! Ahhhhh!"

With that encouragement, I let loose a hot stream of cum into her wet pussy, filling up her vaginal vault, and as I pumped away, the cum oozed out her vagina and ran down to her asshole.

I groaned loudly and lowered her legs as she squeezed my butt cheeks as if to wring every last drop of semen from me. She stroked my hair tenderly, and when I looked at her, she raised her mouth to kiss me.

Looking at each other with our chests heaving trying to catch our breath, our eyes locked. She smiled and was the first to speak.

"Now THAT was a fuck and a half! Damn, you put some effort into that."

I panted out, "I try to give you a good ride."

"Shit, man! No complaints here! That was awesome. Now get a nap and do that again when I'm sober."

We both laughed.

She patted me on the ass again.

"Let me up, I feel like I am full of cum for some reason. I need a washcloth. Hell, I need a towel!"

She waddled off to the bathroom cupping her hand under her pussy and washed up while I lay back on the bed and tried to catch my breath. After a few minutes, she came back and handed me a damp washcloth to wipe my dick.

"Thanks. I made a mess."

She grinned.

"Yeah, you did. It was worth it."

"You're very vocal tonight in your encouragement."

She laughed.

"Yeah, I got kind of caught up in the moment. Did you mind?"

"No, I liked it. I like to hear how I am doing."

She jumped into bed and lay against me.

"Snuggle with me until I go to sleep, which will not be very long, then let me go."

"You got it."

"Thanks, that's nice. In the morning don't be surprised if I don't kiss and act romantic."

"I understand."

Morning

I woke up and looked around for Darla. She was nowhere to be seen. I went to her bathroom and cleaned up with what I had, borrowing her toothpaste and brushing my teeth with a finger. Stumbling out to the kitchen, I saw her through the window at the barn, carrying what I thought was probably horse feed in buckets. I looked at my watch, it was daylight but early.

Pulling on my shoes, I walked to the barn and greeted her.

"Good morning!'

She looked up and smiled. She had put on cutoff jeans shorts and a tee shirt, with a visor and her sunglasses. It was bright out there.

"Hey! Took you long enough to come help me."

I laughed.

"How long have you been out here?"

She smiled again.

"Not that long. Can you fill the water buckets like you did last night?"

"Sure."

I helped with chores the best I could since I'm a city boy. We got done and started walking back to the house.

"Is there more to load into the trailer?"

She nodded.

"Yeah, but I can do it later. Or you can help if you're still here. Anyway, I want coffee now."

I sat at her big kitchen table and watched her as she made the coffee, then stood against the countertop with her arms crossed over her chest looking at me as the coffee pot gurgled away.

"Last night, just before I went to sleep, I seem to remember coming and then a vigorous finish to the event."

"I recall the same thing."

She shook her head.

"Two of those large daiquiris kicked my ass."

"You deserve a good drinking session now and then, and I was with you to drive you."

She shook her head again.

"I'm glad it was with you. There's no tellin' what another man would have done to me when I passed out."

I smiled at her.

"Last night you said you might have woken up with cum in your mouth, pussy, and asshole."

That got a laugh out of her.

"I said that? Then I wasn't worried about you. Did I really tell you that you could fuck me up the ass? I kinda remember that."

I nodded.

"You did. I told you I'd rather wait until you were sober."

"Thanks. You really are a nice guy."

"That's what I keep telling everyone."

She poured us a cup of coffee and sat down at the table. We sipped our coffee in silence for a while.

I said, "Tell me about yourself, Darla. We haven't talked much."

She laughed.

"No, we haven't. There's not much to tell. I work at the lab in a hospital in Shreveport. I'm just a crazy horse lady who lives way out here by herself. Occasionally I get men to come out here, I make them help me do stuff, fuck them, and then they go away."

I smiled.

"Do you want me to go away?"

"You don't need to go just yet. But don't be offended if I don't call you to come back for a month or more. It takes me a while to get really horny again."

"I'm sure there's more to your story. Were you ever married?"

"Yeah, twice actually. You're Air Force, right?"

I nodded.

She shook her head.

"That's ironic. I came down here from Indiana with an Air Force guy, we were married up there and he got transferred."

"What happened to him?"

"He got transferred again, and we had already moved out here and I didn't want to leave what I thought of as the perfect horse farm. So, I went a little nutty and told him to leave and go on with his assignment. He did."

"Wow. Was that hard?"

"Oh, yeah it was. He was a good guy. He built that barn out there for me all by himself, put up all the fences, ran electrical power and water out there so I didn't have to haul buckets. He worked his ass off to get this place just the way I wanted. Then I told him to fuck off."

She gazed out the window without expression for a minute.

"Now, I'm not very proud of that decision when I look back on it. Like I said, I was a little nutty back then. I spent some time in therapy and am better now. Too late for him, though."

She looked out the window for at least a minute more, then turned to me with a small smile.

"Enough about my crazy ass. What's your deal? Are you married? Is some wife gonna come out here and kick my butt?"

I had to laugh.

"No, not married. I was once, a long time ago. Not doing that again. I'm career Air Force, will probably stay for 30 years the way things have been going."

She nodded.

"When are you due to leave here? How much longer can I have you come help me and of course screw me?"

I shrugged.

"I'm at a headquarters job for at least another year. Then after that, it's a crap shoot. I'd like to go back to supervising troops at the squadron, but everything is pretty stable right now, nobody's moving in my program."

She nodded.

"Good, you can come back here for a while then, if I don't scare you off. Are you tired of screwing me yet?"

"Nope."

"That's good, I like what you do to me. Hell, fucking me standing up, then up against the side of my truck in broad daylight! And last night! I've never been fucked so hard in my life! You are some kind of wild stud."

"I got a little turned on."

She laughed.

"I suppose so. Well, I better fuck you again so you will want to come back. How do you want it?"

She was very straightforward when it came to talking about sex.

I thought for a brief moment.

"How about on the bed, with you on top after another great blow job?"

She smiled.

"I love a man that knows what he wants. Let's kiss on the couch and you can feel me up for a while to get worked up."

"I thought you only liked to kiss when you had been drinking and felt romantic."

She laughed.

"Yeah, and now I am feeling a little romantic! I could tell you like to kiss. Like I said, I'm crazy. Besides, I might be able to come again if you get me all hot and bothered. Kissing might help that. Or not. Who the fuck knows?"

We moved to the living room, sat next to each other, and started kissing. She was really good at it, with her tongue darting around my mouth. I played with her unrestrained boobs under her shirt and tweaked the nipples. She moaned a little. I put my other hand down to her shorts and unbuttoned them, noticing there were panties this time as I put my fingers on her labia. I needed more access.

"Can you stand up so I can slide your shorts off?"

"Sure."

She did, and I slid the shorts off, kissing her thighs as I did so. She was in a hurry.

"Might as well get naked while we are here."

She pulled her tee shirt off and tossed it aside, standing naked in front of me. I ran my hands up and down her torso, ass, and legs, squeezing her boobs and then I kissed her all over. She reached for my shirt and pulled it off over my head, then unfastened my shorts and pushed them down, pulling my dick out and giving it a stroke.

I had her sit on my lap with her legs to one side, with her arms around my neck. I could reach lots of fun stuff that way. As we kissed, I reached between her legs and spread them a little so I could play with her pussy. As my finger went into her vaginal vault, she gasped and moaned, then went back to kiss me passionately. I was getting pretty worked up.

I turned her so her back was to me and her legs were spread outside of mine. I had great control of her pussy and boobs, and she lay her head against my neck and moaned as my finger entered her again and massaged her G spot. My cock was sticking up between her thighs, and she stroked it into even greater stiffness.

Darla was squirming and groaning, and I kept up my finger action while I played with her nice boobs, kissing her on the side of the neck. After a few minutes, she gasped out a request.

"Let me blow you now, I'm getting hot as shit!"

"Okay."

She got off me, turned around, and took me in her mouth while she knelt on the floor. It was a great feeling. Her tongue went around the shaft and back to the head, circling the glans. She then bobbed her head up and down, experimenting with how far she could take me down her throat without gagging. All that was making me as hard as a rock. She could tell.

Smiling up at me, she said, "Ready to go to the bedroom?"

"That is a yes."

We stood, and I embraced her with my cock poking her in her stomach as we kissed some more. Then I surprised her by picking her up in my arms and carrying her to the bedroom as she wrapped her arms around my neck and kissed me. I set her gently on the bed.

She was grinning.

"How romantic! That was cool!"

I got my head down between her legs and started licking her slit up and down, noting the pungent aroma of fucked pussy. I had come in there last night and it had not been cleaned. It was different, not bad, so I pressed on and gave her hole a lick and then sucked her clit as she squirmed and moaned.

She realized that as I was eating her pussy and had a comment.

"I'm sure I'm not too fresh down there, I didn't know you were going to go down on me."

"It's okay, not to worry."

"Kiss me so I can see what I taste like."

She was a nut case. I rose to kiss her, and her tongue explored mine for a minute.

"Hmmm. Different than last night. As long as you aren't grossed out, I'm good."

I went back to her clit, then shifted up between her legs.

"Slight change of plans. I want to fuck you with me on top for a minute, then I'll put you on top."

"Okay, just not too hard. I'm a little sore from last night."

"I'm sorry, honey. I'll take it easy."

She patted my ass as I lined up to enter her.

"It's okay, I wanted it like that and loved the shit out of it."

Her hand lined me up, and I pushed in. With all the licking and foreplay, my cock went right in, and she groaned as I went all in. Her pussy felt great, the tightness was just right, and the walls were supple and smooth. It was damned good pussy.

I started a gentle but long stroke into her, and she pushed her hips into me gently as I did so. She caressed my ass, legs, and back as I did so, and made happy sounds of moaning and groaning as her eyes closed. After a few minutes, I wanted her on top.

"I'm going to roll on my back and have you get on me."

She nodded her head enthusiastically. I got on my back, and she straddled me, sliding my cock in her as she lowered herself and exclaimed her pleasure.

"Ahhh! That's nice."

She braced herself with her hands on my shoulders and started rocking her hips back and forth, having fun but being careful not to sit down too hard on her bruised pussy. After a few minutes, she was getting worked up but not ready to come. I decided to give her some mentoring.

"Push your clit against me, like you're trying to scrub my pubic hair off with your clit."

She tried that motion and liked it.

"Oh, yeah. That's good."

I put my hand up in front of her pussy.

"Now push my hand away by pushing forward with your hips."

She tried that.

"Mmm. That's even better. I'm really close now!"

I reached around her ass and circled her anus with my finger. She looked me in the eye.

"Push it in! Put your finger in my ass!"

I got some lubrication on my finger from the pussy juice and saliva and gently pushed my finger up her ass. She moaned loudly.

I then reached for her boobs and licked and nibbled on the nipples. She started to come.

"Ahh shit! Oh, fuck! Ahhhhh! Yes! Oh, yes! Oh, man! Push hard into me! I'm coming! Ahhhh!"

With that, she tossed her head back and cut loose with a loud shout of pleasure.

"FUCK! OH YEAH, FUCK! OH SHIT, THAT FEELS SO FUCKING GOOD!"

Then her back arched and she sat straight up and closed her eyes as the orgasm finished. She shivered and opened her eyes and gasped.

"Oh, that was nice! What a great idea. Now we have to get you to come. What do you want to do?"

"How about if I roll you over and finish that way?"

She was breathing heavily but nodded her assent. I pulled my finger out of her ass and rolled us over, staying inside her. I started a gentle long thrust rhythm and was enjoying that when she wanted more.

"Go ahead and do it harder!"

"I don't want to hurt you, Darla."

"Fuck it, it's not that bad and it hurts in a good way."

I ramped up the activity, watching her face. She winced a few times but did not complain. Then she had another idea.

"Pull your dick out! I'll blow you and you can come in my mouth!"

This was a major change from yesterday when she wanted the taste of dick out of her mouth.

"Are you sure?"

"Yes, damn it! Get that dick up here before I change my mind!"

I pulled out and moved up her torso so she could blow me. She raised up on her elbows and took me into her mouth, pussy juice and all.

She started the oral job with her tongue wrapping my shaft, then made it even better by taking me even farther down her throat than she did before. After a very short time, I was ready to blow.

"I'm about to come!" I cried out, giving her one last chance.

She responded by increasing the rate of sucking and I lost it, coming in a huge torrent of cum in her mouth and down her throat. She kept up the action as spurt after spurt of semen went into her mouth, on her teeth, and down her throat. Stopping, she licked the last dribble from the head of my dick and grinned up at me with a little drop of cum oozing out the corner of her mouth.

"How was that?"

"That was fantastic! How was it for you?"

She shook her head.

"Pretty gross. I need to get up and wash this crap out of my mouth."

I got off her. She trotted to the bathroom, where I heard spitting and water running. She came back with a neutral expression on her face.

"That wasn't too bad. Some of it went down my throat and I swallowed it. Now I can say I'm a cum swallowing crazy lady! Kiss me, I used mouthwash."

I did, secretly hoping all the cum was gone. She pulled back and looked at me seriously.

"That's the first time I have done that. I never have let a man cum in my mouth, though many have wanted to, even my husband. That's your special treat to keep you coming back."

I stroked her hair.

"Thanks, Darla. I appreciate it."

"You're welcome. By the way, nobody has ever stuck a finger up my ass, either. Okay, we have both sucked, fucked, and come. Help me finish loading the trailer and then I'll feed you leftover pizza and kiss you goodbye."

I had to laugh.

"Am I being excused?'

She grinned.

"That's a nice way of saying it. I'll be calling you again to help me with farm chores and bedroom chores, probably before a month is out. You have moved to the top of my list of helpers."

As I pulled my clothes on, I was already looking forward to the next time I would be invited to the farm. I hoped it would be soon.

Don't miss out!

Visit the website below and you can sign up to receive emails whenever Dirk Caldwell publishes a new book. There's no charge and no obligation.

https://books2read.com/r/B-A-UHDZ-PYVKC

BOOKS 2 READ

Connecting independent readers to independent writers.

Did you love *A Visit to the Farm with Darla - a Sexy Short Story*? Then you should read *Back to the Farm with Darla - A Sexy Sequel*[1] by Dirk Caldwell!

[2]

Dirk always weaves a story in with the sex scenes. This novel will appeal to men and women.

Air Force Enlisted man Dirk goes back to visit his friend Darla at her farm. She fulfills several fantasies and together they form a long-lasting relationship. The sex is wild and exploratory, with each character performing acts they would not have imagined. A sad yet romantic ending makes the reader feel as if they were a part of the action.

---

1. https://books2read.com/u/mVel62

2. https://books2read.com/u/mVel62

Also by Dirk Caldwell

Adventures of Stan
Stan Does a Big Girl and Gives her a Big Orgasm
Stan Does a Female Police Officer While On Duty
Stan Scores on a Booty Call with Barbara
Stan Takes Barb's Anal Cherry
Stan Teaches Oklahoma Karen About Sex in the City
Stan gets Kinky with Barb on Vacation
Barb Wants more Orgasms with Stan before She gets Engaged to
Another Man
Stan Does Barbara's Mom!
Stan Titty Fucks Barbara's Friend!
A Stopover in Eufaula to Fuck Lynn Again
Stan Shows a Redhead How to Have an Orgasm
Liz loses Her Anal Cherry during a Three Way
Stan has Sex with a Black Chick!
Stan Has Sex with a Pregnant Woman!
Stan Sport Fucks a Sexy Lawyer!
Stan Titty Fucks Traci's Grandma!
Stan Titty Fucks His Art Dealer!

Dirk Caldwell Romantic Erotic Novels
A Visit to the Farm with Darla - a Sexy Short Story
A Layover in Omaha with Tina
A Night in Eufaula with Lynn
A Trip to the Lake with Kim
Older Women need Love, too! Erika visits Atlanta
Lessons in Love: Gabriella Visits Indianapolis
Big Girls Need Love, too! Barbara from Kokomo
Flight Attendants want Love: Flying High with Jessica
Back to the Farm with Darla - A Sexy Sequel
Redheads Need Love: Megan From New Orleans
A Big Girl finds Love: Joann from Shreveport
Lust from London: My Affair with a British Nymphomaniac
Paula's Sexy European Weekend
Mother and Daughter Threesome

Dirk Caldwell Sexy Short Stories
To All the Girls I've Loved Before: Sexy Short Stories Book 1
To All the Girls I've Loved Before: Sexy Short Stories Book 2
To All the Girls I've Loved Before: Sexy Short Stories Book 3

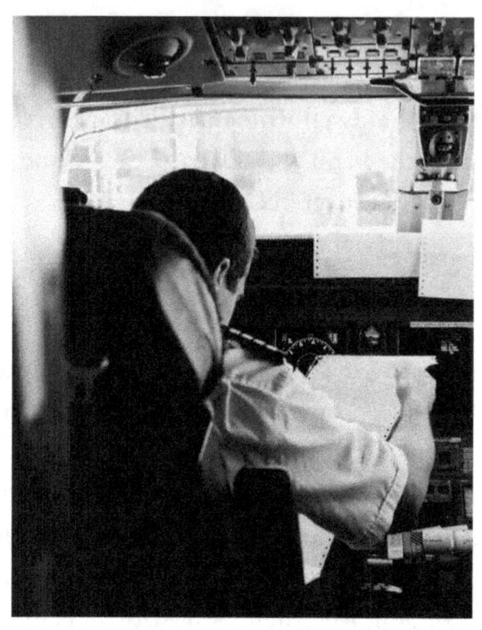

About the Author

Dirk Caldwell is the pen name of the author of an erotic book series. Dirk embodies the life experiences of the author as an Air Force veteran and commercial airline pilot. Most of the content is true and relates to the author's experiences. It's up to the reader to decide what is fiction and what is true life.